Three and a Witch

Chapter Readers

'Three and a Witch'
An original concept by Lou Treleaven
© Lou Treleaven 2021

Illustrated by Vicky Lommatzsch

Published by MAVERICK ARTS PUBLISHING LTD

Studio 11, City Business Centre, 6 Brighton Road,

Horsham, West Sussex, RH13 5BB

© Maverick Arts Publishing Limited November 2021

+44 (0)1403 256941

A CIP catalogue record for this book is available at the British Library.

ISBN 978-1-84886-846-5

www.maverickbooks.co.uk

This book is rated as: Grey Band (Guided Reading)

Three
and a
Witch

Written by
Lou Treleaven

Illustrated by
Vicky Lommatzsch

Chapter 1

Aunt Spyte had vanished. There was no doubt about that. With a great big bang, she had fizzled away in a puff of purple smoke. Only her stripy socks were left, hanging out of her cauldron. The three of us stood there, staring in disbelief.

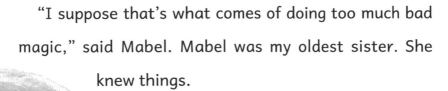

"I suppose that's what comes of doing too much bad magic," said Mabel. Mabel was my oldest sister. She knew things.

"Maybe it was because I didn't clean the cauldron properly?" asked Eva, my next oldest sister. She worries about things.

"Of course it wasn't," said Mabel, but she looked a bit thoughtful after that. Bits of old potions were stuck to the inside of the cauldron,

splattered over the big spell book and slopped all over the floor. "We should clean up."

"Not me," I said, sitting on a three-legged stool and folding my arms. As the youngest I'm sometimes stroppy—it's part of the job. "Aunt Spyte isn't here to boss us around anymore."

"Do you want eye-of-newt and toe-of-frog all over the floor while you're having breakfast, Clemmy?" Mabel asked.

I didn't, so I picked up a broom and helped. As usual, the broom did a little quiver when I touched it as though it wanted to take off. I expect sweeping up is very boring for a witch's broom.

"What about *those*?" Eva asked with a quavering voice.

Aunt Spyte's stripy socks were still in view. As we watched, the cauldron gave a shudder and there was a final purple fizzle. The last bit of Aunt Spyte was gone.

Aunt Spyte's cat, Shadowcurse, rose from his windowsill bed, jumped down and hissed fiercely at the cauldron. We jumped back and he scowled round at us as though this was all our fault.

"That's the end of her," said Mabel.

"But what are we going to do?" wailed Eva.

"We're free," I told her, putting down the broom. "And we're three. Not three and a witch anymore. Just three."

Eva looked doubtful. We had been ruled by Aunt Spyte for so long, it was hard to imagine anything else.

"We'll have to do things properly," said Mabel. "The housework, the cooking. I'll make a chart."

"What about money?" That was Eva of course.

"We don't need to worry about that—look!" I pointed up at the shelves where rows of Aunt Spyte's potions sat, all different sizes and colours with labels written in Aunt Spyte's scratchy hand. All waiting for her customers from the village to come and buy them. "And when they're finished, we can make some more."

"No, Clemmy!" Mabel cried. "We're not having anything to do with magic. It's dangerous. Look what happened to Aunt Spyte."

There was a pause as we all remembered.

"Shadowcurse is good at catching rats," Eva suggested. "We could rent him out."

Shadowcurse looked even more furious than usual.

"Maybe not," Eva added.

Just then there was a knock at the door. "Witch Spyte? Witch Spyte? Are you at home?" called a deep voice.

We looked at each other. Aunt Spyte had always made us hide from customers. Mabel shook her head warningly. I jumped up and opened the door.

Chapter 2

A large man with a floury white apron came into the kitchen. "Is the witch at home?" he asked.

We looked at the cauldron and back at each other.

"She's... out," said Mabel, which I thought was rich as she had always told us not to tell lies.

"Can we help instead?" I asked eagerly.

"Maybe you can. I'm here to collect a potion."

"Which one?" I asked before Mabel could stop me.

"Can't remember. The witch said it would help my business. I'm a baker, you see."

I dragged a stool up to the high shelves where the prepared potions were kept and began to read the labels.

"Potion of Clumsiness, Potion of Rubbery Legs, Wiggly Words Potion…"

"That's the one," said the baker.

"But how will a Wiggly Words Potion help your business?" Mabel asked, glaring at me as I lifted down a murky purple bottle.

"I've always been the only baker in Littlevale. Now there's another one. The witch promised it would help me get ahead of my rival."

Mabel looked really disapproving at this, but we had to make the sale if we needed money.

"That will be two gold coins, please," I told him, trying to sound business-like.

"Two? She said it would be three. Very kind of you, I'm sure." The baker took the potion and examined it greedily. "Thank the witch for me, won't you?"

"We will," Mabel said. As the door closed behind him her expression changed. "Oh, I do hate lying."

"Then why did you?" I asked.

"I didn't know what else to say! But I don't like it. And I don't like selling these potions. Wiggly Words? What's that going to do?"

"Does it matter? We have two gold coins now," I said, rattling them.

"We could have had three, Clemmy," Eva pointed out, but I pretended to ignore her.

"It matters because we're responsible for everything that happens now," Mabel said. "And I don't want to do bad things. Do you?"

"No," I admitted.

"No," joined in Eva.

Shadowcurse hissed. He obviously *did* want to do bad things. Or maybe he was hungry because no one had given him his breakfast.

"Let's all eat," said Mabel, noticing the hiss, "and then we'll decide what to do."

We had the best breakfast ever of cheese on toast and we let Shadowcurse have a little bit of cheese too so he wouldn't hiss at us. We all felt better after that and Shadowcurse washed and went to sleep on the windowsill again.

The rest of us had a meeting. We agreed that we would see what the baker's potion did. If it was bad, we would stop selling it. We had two gold coins to spend so we could visit the village for supplies tomorrow and check out the effects of the potion at the same time.

"Can we take the broom?" I asked, but Mabel said no: we might break our necks.

Chapter 3

It was odd without Aunt Spyte and even odder that we spent our first night of freedom sleeping in the cold, damp cellar as we always had done. Shadowcurse stood outside the door like a guard. It was as though Aunt Spyte had trained him to watch over us.

When we got up and realised we could have cheese on toast for breakfast, and cheese on toast whenever we liked, we began to feel differently. Mabel carried on tidying up, Eva brought up all our things from the cellar and made a nice bedroom den for us under the kitchen table, and I leafed through Aunt Spyte's enormous old spell book, until Mabel told me off.

"You could help, Clemmy," she grumbled.

I looked for the broom but this time it was hiding, so the broom and I had a great game of hide-and-seek until Mabel said the chores were done thanks to her and Eva, and it was time to go into the village with our money.

"Shadowcurse is following us," Eva remarked as we walked through the twisty path that led out of the woods.

"He can't stop us," said Mabel firmly.

"He can hiss at us and bite our ankles," I reminded her.

"Walk faster then."

We walked faster and soon reached the village, where Shadowcurse sat under the village sign and glared at us.

"He'll get bored and go home," Mabel said hopefully.

There were so many shops and stalls in Littlevale that we wandered around, dazed. We'd always had too many chores to have time to go out. Having our own money to spend on ourselves was so overwhelming it was almost impossible to make a decision. Mabel wanted to buy a new broom.

"You can't clean properly with a witch's broom," she pointed out.

I couldn't disagree with that, but I had a feeling the broom wouldn't be too pleased to be replaced, even if it didn't like sweeping.

Eva wanted to buy some material and stuffing to make pillows—nice plump thick ones, not the flat ones Aunt Spyte made us use. But what good were pillows when you had an empty stomach?

"We don't need currant buns," Mabel said when I asked her, but her tummy rumbled all the same. "Alright, but don't go mad."

The bakery had a queue and our tummies were almost deafening us as well as everybody else by the time we got to the front.

"How is the potion working?" Mabel asked the baker.

"Business is booming!" he replied, twisting the paper bag of buns and handing it over. "Tell the witch I'll have three more potions."

"Oh no!" whispered Eva.

We munched our buns as we walked through the village. Soon we passed a small, neat little shop with a pretty arrangement of baked goods in the window.

"This must be the rival bakery," Mabel said. "Let's see what they've got."

We started reading the labels propped in front of the food, but as we did so, the letters wriggled and changed.

"Chocolate Slug Cake, Beetle Tart, Apple Fly, Four Ant Buns—yuck!" Eva exclaimed. "Somehow they don't look so nice after all."

A woman in a pretty chequered apron stepped outside. "You're just like the rest," she said bitterly. "Promising to come and buy and then sneering at my efforts. I've a good mind to visit that witch I've heard about and make people regret how they've treated me!"

"Oh please don't!" cried Eva. "It's not their fault."

"I heard there was bad blood in this village, but I didn't believe it until now. I may as well give up." The woman went inside, slamming the door after her.

"The Wiggly Words Potion!" I whispered.

"It's all our fault," said Mabel.

Chapter 4

None of us knew what to say. We walked away slowly and Shadowcurse led us back into the woods. He was the only one who seemed cheerful for once.

"I suppose we did know Aunt Spyte was wicked," Mabel said after a while.

"We never really thought about it before," said Eva. "We were too busy doing her chores and dodging her curses."

"We can't sell any more potions," Mabel said firmly as we entered our clearing. "If a customer comes, we'll just turn them away."

Outside the witch's cottage, there was a queue of villagers.

"Oh dear," Mabel sighed.

"We've been here for ages," grumbled a woman at the back of the queue, hoisting a crying baby up on her hip. "You should serve us first."

"Don't you try and jump the queue! You'll have me to answer to if you do!" shouted a man at the front, shaking his fist.

The whole queue started insulting each other. Mabel stood bravely in front of them. "I'm afraid Aunt Spyte—I mean, Witch Spyte—has vanished."

"Yes, but what about our potions?" said the first man. "I can see them all in the window."

It seemed even the witch's disappearance couldn't stop the villagers. Mabel, Eva and I huddled round.

"We could just sell the ones we've got left," I whispered. "They'll have to give up coming after that."

"But some of those potions are horrible!" argued Eva.

"We could mix the horrible ones with the less horrible ones so they're all just slightly horrible," I suggested.

"We don't know how to do that, Clemmy," Mabel said. "And the effects could be dangerous."

"Hurry up!" shouted several people.

"I ordered my potion months ago, and you can't stop me having it," said an old lady, threatening us with her stick.

We had no choice. To a chorus of complaints we hurried in. Mabel served the customers while I climbed about on the shelves finding the right bottles. Eva went between us. She was very nervous and broke two potions, making the floor sizzle and all three of us sprout long floppy ears for the next hour. All the potions seemed very spiteful and the nasty effects were all aimed at other people in the village.

A young man bought a potion to make his ex-girlfriend grow a tail for a week. A cross woman collected a Braying Potion that would make her gossiping neighbour sound like a donkey. And a lazy man bought a Potion of Sluggishness for his boss so he wouldn't have to go to work early in the morning.

"Good riddance," Mabel said after she shut the door after the last one. "Why are people so horrible round here?"

"Maybe because they have a witch?" I suggested. "You do look funny with donkey's ears, Mabel."

"Do you think people will be nicer when the potions are gone?" Eva asked. She was sitting on Shadowcurse's windowsill with him, which I had never seen anyone else do without getting hissed at.

"Maybe. Or maybe they'll be worse. I think we should make some more," I said, crossing the kitchen to look at the spell book and slipping on the spilt liquid that made us grow ears.

"Clemmy!" Mabel exclaimed.

"I meant nice ones."

"No magic. I mean it."

Another pair of ears sprouted from my head.

"And you can stop that as well!"

Chapter 5

Eva painted a large sign that said 'Closed Due to Witch Vanishment' and Mabel hung it on the front of the house. For the next few days, people turned up, stared at it for a few moments and then walked away, muttering. A few tried banging on the door, but we hid under the table in our den until they had gone. After we had done this a few times, I felt a soft brush against my leg.

"Shadowcurse is under here."

"Don't move and he probably won't bite you," Mabel warned.

We all stayed still except Eva, because the next thing we heard was a hoarse rumbling.

Eva laughed. "It's Shadow purring. Look, I'm stroking him."

We all stared in the dim light under the tablecloth. The fearsome Shadowcurse was sitting on Eva's lap.

"Now that Aunt Spyte is gone, he's not a witch's cat anymore," Eva said happily. "All he really wants is a lap. I think that was why he was so angry at us."

Shadowcurse, or Shadow as we decided to call him, wasn't the only thing that changed. Our fortunes did as well. It wasn't long before we had spent nearly all the money from the potions. It turned out keeping a house going—plus feeding three hungry children and a cat on cheese on toast—was not cheap.

Meanwhile, things in the village had gone from bad to terrible and it was our fault. The new baker had stolen the old baker's blackboard and written rude things on it. The girl who now had a dog's tail had dug up her ex-boyfriend's vegetable garden. And the woman who now brayed like a donkey, thanks to her neighbour, was braying at six o'clock in the morning to wake everybody up early—which wasn't going down well with the lazy man at all.

While Mabel tried to dig the garden and Eva tamed Shadow, I spent all the spare minutes I had examining Aunt Spyte's spell book. I felt sure there could be an answer here to the problems in the village. It was a huge

old tome and very hard to turn the pages—especially as they were covered with splatters from all sorts of ingredients. Most of the splatters were so foul I didn't want to know what they were.

One day, I tried to turn over a particularly sticky page. This had to be the potion Aunt Spyte made the most, but I couldn't work out what it was. Grabbing a damp cloth I carefully began to remove the grime until I uncovered the name of the recipe. It was an Unfriendship Potion.

The instructions said the ingredients made one vial, but Aunt Spyte's scrawled handwriting showed that she had made five hundred vials, enough for everybody in the village!

Could this recipe explain the way the villagers behaved to each other? And could Aunt Spyte have used it as a way of ensuring they stayed angry at each other and bought her wicked potions forever more?

I almost called out to the others, but stopped myself.

Maybe if I studied the instructions I could work out a way to reverse it and make a Friendship Potion! Mabel wouldn't like it. She didn't approve of my interest in magic. But I had secretly watched Aunt Spyte so many times that I thought I could have a go.

Carefully, I wiped the rest of the page. The 'Un' wiped clean away, changing the title of the recipe to 'Friendship Potion'. Before my eyes, the ingredients in the recipe changed. I realised that I wouldn't have to reverse the potion at all! It was going back to the way it was before wicked Aunt Spyte changed it. My hands trembled as I ran my finger down the new ingredients list.

"Clemmy! What are you doing?" demanded Mabel, coming up behind me.

Chapter 6

"Look!" I said excitedly. "This isn't a wicked witch spell book at all! It's just a spell book."

"Just a spell book?" Mabel put her hands on her hips. "Magic is dangerous, Clemmy."

"It is if you don't know how to use it. And I do. I've been watching Aunt Spyte for years." I pointed to the Friendship Potion. "She changed this and used it to poison the villagers against each other. We could use it to make them friends again." As I spoke, Shadow gently butted against my leg. "I think someone agrees with me," I added hopefully.

Mabel thought for a moment. "Aunt Spyte always made us do things we didn't want to do. So from now on we will always put things to a vote."

"I vote yes," I said immediately.

"I vote yes," said Eva. "Shadow thinks it's alright too."

Mabel sighed. "In that case, I agree. But please be careful, Clemmy. I don't want you to vanish too. And if it works, promise me: no more magic."

I pretended I didn't hear. Fizzing with excitement, I noted down the ingredients and went into Aunt Spyte's herb garden to see what I could find.

Aunt Spyte's garden was no use at all. It turned out ingredients for friendship were things you could find anywhere: like a seed blown from a dandelion clock;

a daisy gathered at noon; a gift from a friend (I used a cat hair Shadow left on me); and the breath from a burst of laughter. For 'something made with love', I used a bit of cheese on toast, and for 'a secret whispered at dusk' I used something I had never told anyone. Shadow heard me whisper, but I knew he wouldn't tell.

Once everything had been added to the cauldron, I stirred it twelve times clockwise and twelve times anticlockwise and left it to simmer for twelve hours. It cooled to the colour of spring sunshine. Mabel helped me pour it into a big bottle. She kept looking at me as though she couldn't believe I'd done it. I was pretty proud of myself too.

"But how shall we give it to them, Clemmy?" Mabel asked. "We can't just hand out the potion and tell people to drink it."

"We could put it in something nice," I suggested. "We could call it Sunshine Juice."

"But I still don't know how we could get everybody to drink it," Mabel said.

"I know!" Eva jumped up excitedly. "Let's have a street party in the village!"

"A street party? That could be disastrous! The villagers hate each other," said Mabel.

"Not once they've drunk Sunshine Juice," Eva pointed out.

"Could we organise a party?" Mabel wondered.

"We've got this far on our own. I think we can do anything!" I said, jumping up too.

Eva and I joined hands and danced around the room while Mabel and Shadow looked on uncertainly.

"Alright," said Mabel, finally smiling as we took her hands and made her join in. "Eva, you can make a sign. I'll plan some food. Clemmy, you can think of some games."

"Tug of war!" I shouted. "Egg and spoon!"

Maybe it would work. Maybe it wouldn't. There was only one way to find out.

Chapter 7

The day of the street party was the nicest of the year so far. At first we had trouble persuading people to come, but Mabel had had the bright idea of telling them it was a sort of farewell to Aunt Spyte, and then people felt they had to come.

We also said there would be lots of free food and drink. The villagers weren't used to kindness. It turned out the last party they had been invited to was when the witch moved here thirteen years ago. There had been a lot of free drink then as well.

"Bound to be a catch," murmured at least one person.

There was, but we didn't tell them that.

Mabel was in charge of welcoming people and encouraging them to get a drink. My games would make them hot and thirsty too. That left Eva in charge of the Sunshine Juice stall.

sunshine juice

She had to add the potion to the lemonade we had made, stir it in thoroughly and ladle it into cups. Shadow would be lounging under the table giving her support from below.

Luckily, nature was on our side. It was a blisteringly hot day and the first thing any of the villagers did was rush to the Sunshine Juice stall for a huge drink.

After that things went perfectly. Everyone enjoyed Mabel's cheese on toastlets (bite-sized pieces of cheese on toast, expertly cooked) and I'd added a little twist to the games to make them extra fun.

"We should do this every year!" cried a man as he came second in the Leg and Spoon race (run to keep up with your hovering egg). I recognised the baker, and the winner was the woman who had set up the rival bakery and ruined his blackboard. "Well done," he said, shaking her hand. "Makes a change from baking bread. I never get away from that stove."

"Do you need any help?" the woman asked. "I'm a baker too. I tried to set up my own business, but..."

The man grasped her hand again. "I'm so sorry. I thought there wasn't room for two bakers in the village. But maybe there is. Or perhaps we could join forces—what do you think?"

The two bakers left for the cheese on toastlets stall, deep in discussion about their new business plan. They joined the queue after the young man who had bought a potion from us. He seemed to be reunited with his sweetheart, who had forgiven him. She still had a tail, but it was wagging.

"I think it's working," Mabel said excitedly, coming up behind me.

"Mabel! Clemmy!" Eva was running towards us looking tearful. "It's all gone wrong. Something terrible has happened!"

Chapter 8

"What?" we both gasped.

"Well, when everyone arrived they were so thirsty that I got all flustered and dished out all the drinks and... I forgot to put the potion in!" Eva sobbed.

"What?" I cried.

We looked at each other, then at all the villagers enjoying themselves, laughing, chatting and playing games, then back at each other.

"I think," said Mabel slowly, "the magic has happened anyway."

"All that effort wasted," I sighed.

"Not at all," Mabel said firmly. "The party has been a marvellous success."

"But the potion!"

"We can keep it in reserve. You know, in case things go wrong again."

"But I wanted to use magic!" I bit my lip. It was time to share the secret I had whispered at dusk, the one only Shadow knew. "Mabel, Eva, I've got something to tell you. I'm a—"

"A witch?" Mabel and Eva both said, smiling.

"How did you know?"

"You're the only one of us who's ever been interested in magic," Mabel said. "Or the spell book. And the only one of us who could have made the Friendship potion. And don't think I didn't notice your little tricks on the games."

She pointed to an egg and spoon that were floating in mid-air, and a sack that was waddling off by itself.

"I just thought I'd make it more fun for people," I muttered.

Mabel took my hands. "I'm not angry, Clemmy. If this is who you are, then it's who you are. We haven't changed either. We're still your sisters. And your best friends. And you've shown me you only want to use your powers for good."

"So are we three and a witch again?" Eva asked.

"Three and a witch?" I repeated.

"Mabel, me, Shadow and you," Eva replied.

I looked down at Shadow, who was winding around between our legs, purring loudly. He wasn't a witch's cat anymore. Or maybe he was a good witch's cat now. And I was a good witch. We had helped the villagers to be friends again, and undone all of Aunt Spyte's nasty work.

"Can we open the witch's shop and sell potions again?" I asked.

"I don't think so," Mabel said. "We don't need them anymore."

"What about some other spells?" I asked as we walked back to the Sunshine Juice stall. I couldn't wait to try something else. And see if I could fly the broomstick!

"We'll have a good old look through the spell book when we get back, and have a vote," Mabel said, pouring us some Sunshine Juice. "But for today, let's enjoy what we've got."

So we did.

flying cat
potion

45

Discussion Points

1. Who wants to keep using magic when Aunt Spyte disappears?

2. What potion does Clemmy sell to the baker?

a) A Wiggly Words potion

b) A Distrust potion

c) A Slimy Worm potion

3. What was your favourite part of the story?

4. How do the girls plan to make all the villagers happy again?

5. Why do you think Clemmy was so interested in potion making?

6. Who was your favourite character and why?

7. There were moments in the story when the girls had to **make their own decisions**. Where do you think the story shows this most?

8. What do you think happens after the end of the story?

Book Bands for Guided Reading

The Institute of Education book banding system is a scale of colours that reflects the various levels of reading difficulty. The bands are assigned by taking into account the content, the language style, the layout and phonics. Word, phrase and sentence level work is also taken into consideration.

The Maverick Readers Scheme is a bright, attractive range of books covering the pink to grey bands. All of these books have been book banded for guided reading to the industry standard and edited by a leading educational consultant.

To view the whole Maverick Readers scheme, visit our website at

www.maverickearlyreaders.com

Or scan the QR code to view our scheme instantly!

PILLGWENLLY

16/2/22

Maverick Chapter Readers

(From Lime to Grey Band)